BONITA

Don't miss any of these other stories by Ellen Miles!

THE PUPPY PLACE

BONITA

ELLEN MILES

SCHOLASTIC INC.

For Addison

Copyright © 2016 by Ellen Miles
Cover art by Tim O'Brien
Original cover design by Steve Scott

ISBN 978-0-545-85725-3

10 9 8 7 6 5 4 3 2 1   16 17 18 19 20

Printed in the U.S.A.   40
First printing 2016

CHAPTER ONE

"Do you think Aunt Amanda and Uncle James will like my sign?" Lizzie asked her dad as they walked through the airport parking lot. Lizzie held a rolled-up WELCOME HOME banner in one hand and the back of the Bean's jacket in the other. She knew that her little brother would have loved to race through the parking lot — but that wouldn't be safe.

Dad laughed. "They'll love it," he said. He paused near an orange sign. "Section B-3," he said. "Remember that. We're parked in Section B-3."

Amanda was Dad's sister, which was always hard for Lizzie to get her head around. Grown-up brothers and sisters acted very differently than kid brothers and sisters. Aunt Amanda did not have to grab Dad by the jacket to keep him from running into traffic, for example. And Dad did not tease Aunt Amanda the way Charles (Lizzie's other younger brother) teased her — though, according to Aunt Amanda, he used to, back when she and Dad were kids.

Aunt Amanda and Uncle James were coming home from a trip to Puerto Rico. They went on vacation at odd times, when nobody else did. Aunt Amanda owned a doggy day care and overnight boarding center called Bowser's Backyard. Her busiest times were school vacations and holidays, when lots of her regular clients went away and left their dogs to stay with her. There was a long weekend coming up, so naturally Aunt Amanda was on her way home.

During slow times, Aunt Amanda's assistant, Josie, would take care of running Bowser's Backyard — and also house-sit for Aunt Amanda and Uncle James and take care of their four dogs: three mischievous pugs and Bowser, the old golden retriever for whom the business was named. "The eponymous Bowser," Uncle James, who liked big words, always said.

"Dad," Lizzie asked now, as they approached the doors of the airport terminal, "remind me what, um, epa — epin — *eponymous* means."

"You're thinking of Bowser, aren't you?" Dad grinned at her as he held the door for her and the Bean. He'd heard Uncle James say it, too. "It means a person — or a dog, in Bowser's case — who gives their name to something."

"Right," said Lizzie. Of course, she firmly believed that dogs *were* people — or maybe they were even better than people. Lizzie was dog-crazy, just like her aunt. When she grew up, she planned to be A) a vet, B) a dog trainer, C) a doggy day care owner like Aunt Amanda, D) all of the above, or E) anything else to do with dogs. Even now, Lizzie pretty much lived and breathed dogs. She loved to read about them, play with them, train them, and draw them. She and some friends had a dog-walking business. Lizzie had even convinced her parents that the Petersons should become a foster family for puppies, keeping each one just long enough to find it the perfect forever home.

Best of all, she had a dog of her own: Buddy, the sweetest little brown mutt in the world, with his funny half-perked ears and the adorable heart-shaped white spot in the middle of his chest. Buddy had come to the Petersons as a foster puppy — and he had never left. Fostering meant giving up the dogs they took care of, and they all knew that, but Buddy was the exception to the rule. He was part of the family.

"I wish I could have fit Buddy into my drawing," she said to Dad now, as they headed for the escalator. "He should be on the banner, too, but there wasn't room."

"Scator! Scator!" yelled the Bean, pulling her along. Lizzie rolled her eyes, but she and her dad smiled at each other. The escalator was the reason they had brought the Bean to the airport. He got very excited about moving stairs since there weren't any escalators in Littleton, the town where the Petersons lived. The Bean loved to go along whenever anyone went to the airport, and he always wanted to ride the escalator as many times as he could. As they rode now, he grinned, waving at all the people going the opposite way. Then he tugged on Lizzie's hand to ride down and back up again.

"No time! We'll do some more later," Lizzie promised, tugging back. "Right now we have to go meet Aunt Amanda and Uncle James." The Bean burst into tears. Lizzie let Dad pick him up so she could unroll her banner and get ready to hold it up by the window. She wanted Aunt Amanda and Uncle James to see it as soon as they got off the plane.

Lizzie was proud of the banner. Under the words WELCOME HOME she had drawn a huge picture, kind of like a giant cartoon. In it, all three pugs and Bowser were home alone and having the time of their lives, partying in the kitchen. Bowser was standing by the refrigerator — which he had obviously been able to open — handing out giant hams and whole turkeys. The pugs were arranged at the table and on the counters, eating everything in sight. Lizzie knew her aunt would get a huge kick out of the sign.

"Look, look," said Dad, trying to quiet the squalling Bean. "There's the airplane. It's coming along the runway, and it's going to park right there, and everybody's going to get out. Let's watch. Maybe we'll see the pilot!"

The Bean's cries died down as he peered through the window, snuffling and rubbing his nose.

Lizzie handed one end of the banner to Dad. "Can you hold this?" she asked. She stepped away from him so the banner unfurled to its full length, and they held it up to the window.

"There they are," shouted the Bean.

Lizzie peeked around the side of the banner, sure that the Bean was wrong. But he was right. There were Aunt Amanda and Uncle James, walking down the special rolling steps that had been placed against the parked plane. "Why is she wearing her backpack on her front?" Lizzie asked. She waved and jumped up and down to catch her aunt's attention.

"I don't know," said Dad. "But . . . it looks like there's something *in* the backpack. Do you see what I'm seeing? That little black-and-white head? It looks like — no, it can't be. It looks like —"

"It's a puppy!" yelled Lizzie and the Bean together.

CHAPTER TWO

Lizzie waved frantically to her aunt, forgetting to hold up her end of the banner. The sign dropped to the floor, but Lizzie barely noticed. "What's she doing with a puppy?" she asked. Suddenly, nothing else mattered. Aunt Amanda had a puppy strapped to her chest!

Dad shook his head. "I guess we'll find out soon enough," he said.

Aunt Amanda and Uncle James disappeared for a moment as they entered the terminal. Lizzie hopped up and down impatiently, and the Bean copied her, stomping small sneaker prints onto the forgotten banner. Now Lizzie stared at the door her aunt and uncle would be walking through. "Come on, come on," she muttered, as if the power of her brain waves might force them to appear more quickly.

"There they are," she yelled. She grabbed the Bean with one hand and Dad with the other and dragged them along. "Aunt Amanda! Aunt Amanda!"

Aunt Amanda waved and smiled, then put a finger to her lips in a "shhh" gesture. She pointed at the backpack, and Lizzie saw that the puppy was nestled deep down now, probably sleeping.

"She just fell asleep," said Aunt Amanda in a hushed voice as Lizzie approached. "Poor thing. She couldn't seem to settle down during the flight."

Lizzie peered into the backpack. "She?" she asked, trying hard to keep her voice as low as Aunt Amanda's. "What's her name? Where did you get her? What breed is she? Are you keep-ing her?"

Aunt Amanda laughed. "One question at a time, Miss Lizzie," she said, giving Lizzie's shoul-der a squeeze. "Let's go wait for our baggage, and we'll tell you all about it."

They took the escalator again, but this time the Bean hardly seemed to care. He let Dad carry him so he would be high enough to peer down at the puppy sleeping inside Aunt Amanda's backpack.

They sat on red plastic chairs in the baggage claim area, waiting for suitcases to start appear-ing on the carousel. Usually Lizzie loved to watch people's luggage pop out and ride around like kids on a merry-go-round, but today she was focused on her aunt. "So?" she asked. "Tell us!" She tried to peek inside the backpack, but the puppy was curled up small, and all Lizzie could see was some white fur and some black fur. It took all her restraint to keep her from plunging her hands in to pull the puppy out. She couldn't wait to see her and hold her.

"Her name is Bonita," said Aunt Amanda. "She's what they call a 'Sato' down there in Puerto Rico, a stray mutt who lives on the streets, or in an old warehouse, or on the beach. There are lots and lots of Satos on the island."

Uncle James nodded. "It's hard to see," he said. "People abandon these unwanted dogs and they wander around, hungry and sick. We saw them at the beach first. Your aunt wanted to save them all. She started to bring fresh water down so at least they'd have something to drink."

"That's when I met Tía Angela, Auntie Angel," said Amanda, picking up the story. "She runs Sato Friends, a rescue group down there. They catch the dogs, get them healthy enough to travel, then send them to groups up here in the States who find homes for them."

"Did you find Bonita on the beach?" Lizzie asked.

Aunt Amanda shook her head. "She was at the shelter. Tía Angela had been taking care of her for a few months. She was so sick when she first got there. You should see the pictures." Her face crumpled, as if she was about to start crying. "She had mange, and she was so skinny. . . ."

Lizzie had never seen a dog with mange in real life, but she knew what it was: a sickness that made dogs' coats fall out, so they had itchy, dry bald patches all over. "Poor Bonita," she said, reaching in just one finger to gently touch the top of the puppy's head.

"And of course there's her leg," said Uncle James. "The mange is cleared up, and she's gained some weight. She's had all her shots and she's perfectly healthy, but she still can't really walk right."

"What happened to her leg?" Lizzie asked.

"It was broken at some point when she lived on the streets," said Aunt Amanda. "Tía Angela figures she probably got hit by a car. It healed — but it didn't heal right. She needs an operation. That's one of the reasons I brought her home. I have no idea where we'll find the money to pay for her care, but I just had to help this little girl."

The backpack began to move, and suddenly the puppy popped her head over the side and looked Lizzie right in the eye.

"Oh!" said Lizzie. "She's adorable." Bonita was mostly white, with short, soft fur. One of her floppy ears was black, and the other was white. She had a black nose and shiny black eyes.

The puppy struggled to climb out of the backpack. "Oh, no," said Aunt Amanda. "And there's our luggage." She pointed toward the baggage carousel, which had begun to spit out suitcases, duffel bags, and backpacks. "Great timing, Bonita. Why couldn't you have stayed asleep until we were in the car?" Bonita wriggled happily and licked Aunt Amanda's chin.

¿Por favor, puedo salir ahora? Quiero explorer este nuevo lugar y conocer a la gente.[1]

"She's dying to get out. I'll hold her," said Lizzie. She couldn't wait to cuddle this adorable little pup.

Aunt Amanda looked at her. "Okay," she said. "But hold tight. She's a little spitfire, and she doesn't seem to know or care that her leg is

---

[1]*Please, can I get out now? I want to learn about this new place and meet these people.*

messed up. She sure doesn't let it slow her down." Carefully, Aunt Amanda pulled the puppy out of her backpack and set her into Lizzie's waiting arms.

Lizzie felt her heart melt when she looked down at the scrappy little pup. Bonita looked back, her sparkly eyes dancing with excitement. It was obvious to Lizzie that this puppy's hard life had not broken her spirit. "She's so young to have been through so much," she said. "I'm really glad you brought her home. Are you going to keep her?"

"Of course," said Aunt Amanda.

"Absolutely not," said Uncle James at the very same time.

CHAPTER THREE

"So, are they keeping her or not?" Daphne asked.

"She sounds so cute. I can't wait to meet her," said Brianna.

Maria wiped a tear from her eye and shook her head. "Poor little puppy. She's so lucky your aunt found her. What an amazing story."

It was the day after the airport trip, and Lizzie was telling her friends about meeting Bonita. Since they were all almost as dog-crazy as she was, they were fascinated. Lizzie and her best friend Maria had started a dog-walking business, AAA Dynamic Dog Walkers. Then two other friends, Daphne and Brianna, had become partners in it. Now all four of them met every Friday afternoon to talk about the business, get up to date on their clients, and deal with any problems that might have come up.

"Good question," said Lizzie. "And I still don't know the answer. According to Aunt Amanda, they are definitely keeping her. But Uncle James has always said that four dogs in the family is more than enough and they don't need a fifth. So far they have agreed to keep her at least until she can have that operation on her leg. It'll be a while, because first they have to figure out how to find the money to pay for it."

"She sounds really lovable," said Brianna.

"She's a handful, though," said Lizzie. "Even with that twisted leg, my aunt says she gets right in there with all the other dogs at Bowser's Backyard. She's used to being part of a pack —

she lived with about fifteen other dogs on the beach, according to Tía Angela." Lizzie had told the others all about Sato Friends and how they had rescued so many dogs. "Aunt Amanda says she's sassy and that she bosses around dogs twice her size."

"Kind of like I boss you around," Charles said, cruising by the kitchen table and grabbing an apple from the bowl that sat in the middle of it.

"You wish," Lizzie said, ignoring her friends' laughter. Her brother could be so annoying sometimes. She glared at him as he headed out of the kitchen. "Anyway," she said to her friends, "I told my aunt that I would help out at Bowser's Backyard this weekend, and maybe even during the week, after school. She's having a hard time handling all the other dogs plus Bonita. Do you think the rest of you could cover our business clients for a little while so I'll have time?"

"If it's for Bonita, I'm in," said Brianna.

"I guess so," said Daphne.

Maria didn't say anything, and Lizzie realized that her friend had been quiet for a while. "Maria?" she asked.

Maria shook herself. "Sorry, I was just thinking. What you said about your aunt needing to find the money for Bonita's operation: why don't we help raise it?"

Lizzie's eyebrows shot up. It was such a great idea that she was instantly jealous. Why hadn't she thought of that? "Yes!" she said. "Like when we raised the money for Bandit's operation."

"That's how your whole business got started, isn't it?" asked Brianna. She had heard the story of Bandit, an adorable Shih Tzu the Petersons had fostered. He had needed a heart operation, and Lizzie and Maria had decided to raise money for it by walking dogs.

"That's right," said Lizzie. "Now we're a bigger business and we make more money, but we still give a lot of it away. I know Ms. Dobbins really appreciates what we donate to Caring Paws. If we want to raise money, we'll have to think of another way."

"That's exactly what I was thinking," said Maria. "Plus, I think we should raise money for Sato Friends and help all the other abandoned dogs on the island."

Lizzie's eyebrows shot up even further. Maria was on fire today. So many great ideas. "Absolutely," she said. "So what did you have in mind?"

"I saw these really cute dog beds online," Maria said. "Like, made out of fleecy material with paw print designs or holiday themes. The material isn't expensive. You stuff them with cedar shavings so they smell good and keep fleas away. They're easy to sew, and we could sell them for a good price." Maria loved crafting of any kind, and she was good at it. Once, she had even made a marionette, a puppet whose arms moved when you pulled strings.

"Sewing?" Charles breezed through the kitchen again, this time to get a treat for Buddy, who followed at his heels. He laughed. "Good luck, Lizzie."

Lizzie slumped in her chair, her arms crossed. She stuck out her tongue at Charles. It wasn't that she was bad at crafty stuff. She just wasn't that into it.

"Well, I love the idea!" Brianna clapped her hands and bounced in her seat.

"Sounds perfect," said Daphne.

"We could make other things, too," said Brianna. "Like felted balls for puppy toys. My cousin made one for her little Lab puppy. It was so pretty."

"Why couldn't we just have a dog wash again?" Lizzie asked. They'd done that once as a fundraiser. People could bring their dirty dogs in and have them scrubbed and rinsed by a crew of workers. It was messy good fun, and Lizzie liked that kind of thing a lot more than she liked sitting around threading needles and sewing. Or felting, whatever that was.

"I guess we could do that, too," said Maria. "Maybe we could have, like, a whole dog fair, where there are all kinds of activities and things to buy."

Lizzie gave Maria a high five. "Yesss!" she

yelled, as if Maria had hit a home run. "You're full of ideas today."

By the end of their meeting, the girls had come up with a whole page of ideas for their "Dog-A-Thon." Lizzie couldn't wait to tell her aunt and uncle — and Bonita — about their plan.

CHAPTER FOUR

"And we might have a paw-painting booth," Lizzie said. "You know, like Aunt Amanda does as an activity, finger painting for dogs?"

Uncle James just grunted. "Uh-huh," he said as he took clean food and water dishes from a cart and traded them for the dirty ones from the kennel he was cleaning.

Lizzie and her uncle were at Bowser's Backyard the next afternoon, cleaning kennels while the dogs were having some outside time in the big outdoor play area. It wasn't the most exciting work, but Lizzie barely noticed as she tidied one of the larger kennels. She was all wound up about the plans she and her friends had made, and she had been babbling about it to her aunt and uncle all morning. "It's for Bonita," she reminded her uncle, who didn't seem as thrilled about the Dog-A-Thon as she was. "For her operation."

"That's great," said Uncle James. "Really. It's wonderful that you girls want to help." He shook his head. "I feel sorry for that little pup, I really do."

"But?" Lizzie asked. It sounded like there was more to the story.

"But I just don't see how we can keep her, the way your aunt wants to. She's a real ball of fire, that one. I almost hate to imagine how much more trouble she'll be able to stir up once her leg is fixed." Uncle James told Lizzie how tiny Bonita had turned their whole household upside down in just a couple of days. "She gets the pugs all riled up, and the four of them chase each other around, knocking things over. Then Bowser tries to step in and calm things down, and all she does is jump all over him and make him miserable. It's crazy."

"They'll probably calm down once they know each other better, don't you think?" Lizzie asked as she shook out a dog blanket. They were almost done cleaning up, and soon the dogs would come back to their kennels for breakfast.

"That's what Amanda claims," said Uncle James. "But it had better happen fast. I don't know how much longer I can take this. And it's no good for Bonita, either. She forgets her leg is bad when she runs around like that, and then you can tell she's in pain later on."

"What about giving her some downtime in a crate?" asked Lizzie. She knew that a lot of dogs loved to hang out in a cozy crate, like a den.

Uncle James shook his head. "We tried that, but she freaks out. I guess she's just so used to running free."

Lizzie heard barking coming from the playroom, then Aunt Amanda's voice rising over the noise. "Bonita, stop it! Come here. No, no, put that down!"

"Sounds like she's turning things upside down here, too," Lizzie said. She handed Uncle James the broom. "Maybe I should go see if I can help." She hurried down the hall and pushed open the doors to the playroom. "Uh-oh," she said as she took in the scene.

Bonita was dashing around the room, her crooked leg giving her a funny zigzag style. Instead of taking a straight path, she twisted and turned as she limped. Every other dog in the room chased after her as she dodged and darted expertly, weaving ahead of the pack.

¡No me pueden agarrar! ¡Ji ji![2]

"Hoss!" cried Lizzie, recognizing a Great Dane who was a regular visitor to Bowser's. "Easy, boy. Give up — you'll never catch her. Come here."

Hoss ignored her — just like Fiona, a prancing poodle, ignored Aunt Amanda. In fact, not one of the dogs was paying any attention to the humans in the room. They only had eyes for Bonita. Yipping excitedly, they followed her up and down and over and around the brightly colored plastic play equipment.

"She's like the Pied Piper," said Aunt Amanda. "She gets them going, and it's like they can't even hear me." Her face was red from running and yelling, and her hair had come out of its braid.

[2]*Can't catch me! Hee hee!*

"Bonita," Lizzie called. "Come here, girl." She knelt down on the floor and pulled a piece of hot dog out of the baggie in her pocket. She'd had a feeling it would be smart to have good treats with her that day.

The little black-and-white pup trotted toward her, then suddenly got a sparkle in her eye and veered away, slipping straight under Hoss's tall body. She barked happily, with short high yips.

¡Je je! ¿Ves lo que quiero decir? ¡No hay nadie que me pueda agarrar![3]

The dogs who had been following her also veered, and the whole pack galloped off like a herd of cattle. "See what I mean?" asked Aunt Amanda.

[3]*Ha-ha! See what I mean? Nobody can catch me!*

Lizzie couldn't help giggling. "You should put the doggy-cam on her," she said. "That would be quite a video."

Aunt Amanda had a special camera that she could attach to a dog's collar. Her customers loved being able to watch their dogs play while they were at Bowser's.

Exasperated as she was, even Aunt Amanda had to laugh at the idea of a Bonita-cam. "I don't think so," she said. "That's an expensive piece of equipment, and I don't think it would last long around our wild little girl."

"Maybe I should get her on a leash for a while," Lizzie suggested. "She can hang out with me while I finish getting breakfast ready for all the dogs."

"Would you?" Aunt Amanda asked. "That would be great. We need to get these other dogs settled down a little before they eat."

It took a while to catch Bonita and snap a leash onto her collar, but they managed it. Lizzie petted her gently and she settled down almost right away, but her bright eyes roved around and she wagged her tail in excitement.

¿Ahora qué?[4]

"You're ready for anything, aren't you?" Lizzie asked. "Let's go fill some bowls." She headed back to the kennels with Bonita eagerly leading the way.

By the end of the day, Lizzie felt as frazzled as Aunt Amanda looked. Bonita was eager, all right: eager to snarf up food meant for other dogs when Lizzie's back was turned, eager to steal the toys

[4]*Now what?*

their owners had brought to make them feel at home in their kennels, eager to pounce on their beds and shake-shake-shake them until the stuffing came out.

"She sure is a handful," Lizzie said when she found her aunt and uncle in the office/reception area.

"See what I mean?" asked Uncle James.

"Told you," said Aunt Amanda. "She's a feisty one, all right."

Lizzie nodded tiredly. She didn't see how she could handle Bonita plus all the chores she needed to help with at Bowser's that day. She thought for a second. "Maybe it would be easier if she just came and stayed with us for the rest of the weekend," she said. "You wouldn't have my help here, but you wouldn't really need it without Bonita stirring things up."

Uncle James's face lit up. "Yes!" he said.

Even Aunt Amanda agreed that it might be best for Bonita.

Now all Lizzie had to do was convince her parents.

CHAPTER FIVE

It wasn't that hard to talk her family into fostering Bonita. Lizzie called home and talked to Dad
about it first. She knew he'd agree since he'd
already met Bonita and he knew how cute she
was. "Not to mention that she'll only be here for a
long weekend," Dad had said, as they talked it
over. "How much trouble could she cause?" He
promised to convince Mom, and of course Charles
and the Bean were all for it. Bonita went home
with Lizzie that afternoon "for a trial period," and
by the end of the day, everyone was in love with
her — including Buddy.

Mom hardly even got upset when Bonita and Buddy, working together, managed to knock a box of dog biscuits off the kitchen counter and eat almost all of them. "She just looked at Bonita and shook her head and said how hungry the poor thing must have been all that time when she was living on her own," Lizzie told her friends the next day.

They had decided to meet at her house on Saturday for a day of crafting, since Lizzie had promised to keep a close eye on Bonita. Maria's dad had taken her and Brianna shopping the day before, and they had brought over bags of material, cedar shavings, and other supplies for making the dog beds.

Now they all sat in the living room, clustered together on the couch to watch a how-to video on Mom's tablet. "See? After you cut out your squares, you just sew up the sides with it inside out, then turn it right side in, put in the stuffing, and sew up the last side," said Maria. "Easy-peasy."

Lizzie yawned. Sewing was boring. She looked through the bag of material and picked out some dark-blue fleece fabric with yellow stars and moons. "What do you think, Bonita?" she asked, showing it to the little dog, who lay near her feet. Bonita leapt up and snapped at the material, trying to grab it.

¡Me gusta! ¡Me gusta![5]

"Uh-uh," said Lizzie. "No, Bonita." But she couldn't help smiling at the sassy little girl.

"She is so cute," said Brianna.

"How could anybody abandon her?" asked Maria.

[5]*I like it! I like it!*

Daphne reached out to scratch Bonita's head. "She's adorable," she said. "We should use her picture on the flyer for our Dog-A-Thon."

Lizzie had started to thread a needle, but she put it down, picked up the tablet, and opened its camera app. "Hey, girl," she said, then clicked her tongue to grab Bonita's attention. *Snap.* It was the perfect shot: Bonita with her head cocked to one side, eyes bright with curiosity. Lizzie took a whole bunch of pictures as Bonita struck different poses: sitting, doing a play bow to Buddy, lying on her back. "Check it out," Lizzie said, showing them to the girls.

"Nice," said Daphne. "But what about your dog bed?"

Lizzie put down the tablet and picked up her needle and thread. The others were already well into their projects. She finished threading the needle and began to stab it through the material.

"Wait!" said Maria. "You have to cut out your squares first, like on the video."

"I knew that," Lizzie said. "I was just practicing." She picked up the big scissors and began to cut. How could she have paid attention to the video when Bonita was so much more fun to watch? "Right, Bonita?"

Bonita put a paw up on Lizzie's lap, then climbed the rest of the way in, almost pushing Lizzie over. Lizzie laughed as she put the scissors aside. "You're a real lovebug now that you've learned to be around people, aren't you?" she asked.

"Give her this ball I brought," said Brianna. "See if she likes it." Brianna pulled a soft felted ball out of her backpack. Lizzie liked the colors: aqua and purple. When Brianna tossed it to her, Lizzie showed it to Bonita. The puppy grabbed it, jumped up, then ran madly through the living room with Buddy at her heels.

¡Whee! *Nunca tuve ningún juguete. Qué diver-
tido que es esto.*[6]

"Hey, bring that back," said Lizzie. She got
up and chased after Bonita, but the little pup
swerved and ducked and scrambled so quickly
that Lizzie couldn't even get close.

"Over here, Bonita," said Maria, putting her
blanket aside.

Soon all four girls were racing through the
downstairs, shrieking and waving their arms,
chasing one small but very clever dog. Not even
Buddy could get close to her.

"Lizzie!" Mom walked downstairs from her
office, where she'd been working. "You girls really
have to settle down. You're just getting the dogs
more excited."

---

[6]*Wheee! I never had toys before. This is so much fun!*

Bonita must have heard the tone of Mom's voice. She went right over to her and dropped the ball at her feet, looking up at her with happy eyes.

Mom smiled. "You really are a scamp, aren't you?" she asked.

The girls settled back down to their sewing while Bonita and Buddy curled up for a nap nearby. "Ta-da!" Lizzie said, holding up her dog bed. "How about that? I finished ahead of everyone." The bed was a little lumpy and maybe not so square, but it was done, all stuffed with cedar shavings and everything.

Bonita jumped up, grabbed at the bed, and shook it, spraying wood shavings all over the living room.

"Lizzie!" said Maria as she leapt up to get the bed back from Bonita. "You skipped a step. You were supposed to make a liner to put the shavings in."

The girls were still cleaning up the mess when Lizzie heard the phone ring. Mom answered it, and after a few minutes she came into the living room. "I have an announcement," she said. She paused dramatically in the doorway until all the girls looked up at her. "That was your aunt," she told Lizzie. "You won't believe who's coming to your Dog-A-Thon."

CHAPTER SIX

"Who?" asked Lizzie. "Somebody special?"

Her mom nodded. "Somebody very special." She folded her arms and smiled. "It turns out that your aunt told a friend about what you girls are doing, then that friend told a friend, and that friend told another friend —"

"Mom, who is it?" Lizzie knew her mother was trying to build the suspense, but she couldn't take it anymore. "Just tell us!"

"Well, one of those friends happens to be friends with someone who is friends with —"

"Argh!" Lizzie cried.

"He's a singer . . . and a dancer . . . and so cute and talented . . ." Mom must have seen the face Lizzie was making at her. "Maxwell Martin," she finished quickly.

"Eeeeek!" Daphne screamed. "No way." She jumped up and down, shaking her hands.

Maria screamed, too, then turned white and looked like she was about to faint. "Really?" she whispered over and over. "Really?"

Lizzie's mom grinned. "Isn't it amazing?" she asked. "Maxwell Martin, right here in Littleton."

"I guess that *is* big news," said Lizzie. She wasn't about to scream or jump up and down or faint or anything. She didn't really get what the big deal was about Maxwell Martin. Still, she knew that he was a big star. A huge star, in fact. Everybody in the world knew who Maxwell Martin was.

Well, everybody except Brianna. Lizzie noticed that she just stood there, smiling in a sort of bewildered way. "I guess this guy must be kind of famous," she said. "Like, online."

Now Lizzie understood. Brianna's mom was very strict about her time online. She was allowed to use the computer only a half an hour a day, and only for researching school projects. That meant Brianna never saw cute kitten videos, funny puppy pictures . . . or Maxwell Martin videos.

"He's that guy," Maria said. "You know, the really great-looking one."

"The one with the hat," Daphne said. "And the vest."

"And the smile," Maria said, pretending to swoon. "And that Australian accent."

Brianna shrugged and shook her head. "Sorry," she said.

"He's pretty amazing," Lizzie told her. "He's such a cool dancer — you should see his moves. And he shoots these music videos all over the world, and everywhere he goes he just uses local people for his backup dancers. Like, kids like us."

Maria and Daphne started singing Maxwell Martin's latest song and doing the dance that went with it. *"Every day is my birthday,"* they sang. *"Every day everything is new."* They threw their hands in the air and wiggled their heads.

Lizzie joined in, and then her mom did. *"Every day a new day to spend it all with you,"* they sang, smiling wide as they danced. When they got to the chorus, Lizzie waved Brianna toward her. "Come on, you can do it," she said. *"It's my birthday! It's my birthday! It's my birthday!"* they all sang. Buddy and Bonita jumped around, wagging their tails and barking. All the dancers struck poses as they shouted the chorus again, then collapsed on the floor, laughing.

"His songs just make me feel so happy," said Daphne.

Lizzie grabbed the tablet and did a quick search. "Look," she told Brianna. "Here he is. See? He's dancing with kids in Kenya. And then in Peru, and then in Russia. Isn't that cool? And he always wears that hat. Dad says it's called a bowler."

Brianna nodded to the beat. "I can see why everybody likes him," she said. "Why in the world is he coming to Littleton?"

"Because," Mom said, "apparently he knows all about Satos. He already owns one, named Bliss."

"You're kidding." Lizzie's jaw dropped open. She had read all kinds of things about Maxwell Martin, but this was something she had never heard. "That's amazing."

"I know," said Mom. "So when he heard about the Dog-A-Thon, through a friend of a friend of a friend, he said he wanted to be here for it. At least, that's what your aunt says."

"Everybody is going to totally freak out," said Lizzie. "I can't wait to tell people."

"Oh, I almost forgot," said Mom. "We're not supposed to tell a soul. We're supposed to keep it really quiet for now so it doesn't turn into a giant thing with TV news stations camping out on our lawns."

"But . . . wouldn't giant be good?" Daphne asked. "I mean, for selling things and raising money?"

"There will be plenty of people here, I'm sure," said Mom. "I think you'd better make as many dog beds as you can."

"Speaking of dogs," said Lizzie, "I see Buddy

48

over there by the fireplace, but where is Bonita?" She realized she had not seen the pup since they were all dancing together.

"Uh-oh," said Mom. "I thought you were going to watch her."

"I just got so excited about Maxwell Martin," said Lizzie. "But it's only been a couple of minutes. She can't have gone far."

She had not gone far at all. When they searched the house, they found Bonita in the kitchen pantry. The recycling bins had been knocked over, and she was sitting happily on top of a pile of shredded newspaper, chewing on an empty plastic milk container. She looked up at Lizzie and Mom as they glared down at her, her eyes sparkling as if she wanted to let them in on a hilarious joke. She thumped her long, thin tail on the floor and grinned at them.

*¡Me encantan todos los juguetes especiales aquí!
Tía Ángela tenía razón. Este lugar es genial.*[7]

"Oh, Bonita," said Lizzie.

"I have a feeling it's going to be an extra-long long weekend," said Mom.

[7]*I love all the special toys here! Tía Angela was right. This place is great.*

CHAPTER SEVEN

As it turned out, the long weekend with Bonita was shorter than Lizzie had expected. Mom knocked on Lizzie's door first thing on Monday morning. "Lizzie, are you up? Wake up!"

Lizzie groaned. It was a vacation day, a chance to sleep late. She glanced at the clock on her bedside table and groaned again. Next to her, Bonita stirred sleepily.

"Great. *Now* you want to sleep," said Lizzie, giving the dog a kiss on the head. All night, Bonita had been restless in bed next to Lizzie. She had tossed and turned and gotten up and back down again, licked Lizzie's face, licked her own paws, pushed her feet into Lizzie's back, and generally kept Lizzie awake for hours.

"Okay, okay." Lizzie sat up and stretched, yawning. "What's so important, anyway?"

Mom stepped into her room. "Your aunt just called. She wants you to bring Bonita to Bowser's this morning — as soon as you can."

"But why?" asked Lizzie. "I thought we were keeping her for the day."

Mom shrugged. "She wouldn't say. She said it's a surprise, and she wouldn't even tell me. Come on, get dressed. I can drive you over there as soon as you're ready. I have to pick up Charles from his sleepover at David's anyway."

It was hard to stay grumbly with Bonita dancing around. Lizzie pulled on a pair of jeans and grabbed a T-shirt from her drawer. "Okay, little girl," she said as Bonita sniffed at the door. "Let's get you outside, then we'll go see what's up with Aunt Amanda."

Before she left, Lizzie called Maria. "I can't come over to sew dog beds today after all," she told her friend. She explained that her aunt needed her, even though she wouldn't say why.

"It sounds so mysterious," said Maria. "Why won't she tell you?"

"Maybe she convinced Uncle James to keep Bonita, and they want to practice having her around," said Lizzie. "I don't know. But I do know that they probably need my help, since they still have all the overnight dogs."

"I guess we'll just have to manage without you, then," said Maria.

Lizzie sensed something like relief in Maria's voice. "My dog beds weren't *that* much lumpier than everyone else's, were they?" Lizzie asked her friend. The four girls had turned out a lot of dog beds the day before, after they'd settled down from hearing the big news about Maxwell Martin. They'd made Chihuahua-sized ones, cocker spaniel–sized ones, Lab-sized beds, and even a few huge Leonberger-sized beds, in all sorts of colors and designs. Now, on the other end of the line, Maria was quiet. "Well, were they?" Lizzie asked again.

"Um," said Maria.

Lizzie rolled her eyes. "Whatever," she said. "I'll call you later and see how it's going. As soon as we have enough beds in all the different sizes, we should pick a date for the Dog-A-Thon. We have a lot to pull together for this event."

Truthfully, she was relieved, too. She'd had fun hanging out with her friends the day before, but she had not enjoyed the sewing. Her dog beds *were* lumpy and weirdly shaped, and she had stuck herself with the needle more times than she could count, so a couple of the lighter-colored beds even had dark blotches on them where she'd bled from a pricked finger.

"Let's go, Lizzie," Mom said now, coming into the kitchen. "Your aunt seemed to feel it was very important for you and Bonita to get over there as soon as you could." She picked up the keys to the van.

Lizzie said good-bye to her friend and hung up. "Let's go, Bonita," she said, scooping the pup into her arms.

A little later, Mom glanced at Lizzie as they drove to Bowser's Backyard. "You could have at least run a brush through your hair," she said. "I don't think we were in *that* much of a rush."

Lizzie just smiled. "The dogs don't care what I look like," she said. "Right, Bonita?" Bonita, who sat upright on the seat next to Lizzie, gave her a lick on the cheek.

¡Siempre te amaré![8]

Mom dropped Lizzie and Bonita off at Bowser's. "Call when you need a ride home," she said.

Lizzie pushed open the door to the reception area and saw Josie wiping down the counters. "Your aunt's waiting for you," said Josie. "She's in the playroom."

Aunt Amanda was mopping the floor in the play-room while Uncle James ran around, picking up toys and throwing them into a big basket. "You're here," said Aunt Amanda. "Great!" She took a look at Lizzie and shook her head. "You might want to

[8]*I'll always love you!*

tuck in your shirt," she said. "And there's a hair-brush in the bathroom. Hurry. Go do it now. Take Bonita, and keep her out of the way while we get ready."

"Get ready for what?" Lizzie asked, but her aunt just ignored her, waving her away. Lizzie rolled her eyes. Why did it matter what her hair looked like? She headed for the bathroom, which turned out to be sparkling clean, with new paw-print towels on the towel rack. What was going on at Bowser's?

When she emerged from the bathroom, Bowser's Backyard was quiet. The dogs were in their kennels and there wasn't a person in sight. Where was everybody? Lizzie and Bonita walked through the playroom and out to the reception area, which looked tidier than Lizzie had ever seen it. Still not a person around.

Lizzie opened the front door. "What are you all doing out here?" she asked when she saw her aunt and uncle and Josie standing outside.

"Here he comes!" said Aunt Amanda as a shiny black limousine pulled into the parking lot. "It's really true."

The car drew to a stop.

One of the back doors opened.

And out stepped Maxwell Martin.

CHAPTER EIGHT

Lizzie felt her heart skip a beat. Maria was right. He was awfully tall and handsome, and his smile was full of big, bright white teeth. He looked just the way he did on his videos: he was even wearing a bowler. In his arms was a tiny white dog with brown spots and the cutest stand-up ears.

Bonita saw the dog, too. She tugged at her leash, and Lizzie stooped to pick her up. "Easy, Bonita," she said.

"Bonita!" Maxwell Martin looked straight at Lizzie, and her heart skipped about five more beats. "The very girl I came to see." That Australian accent really was adorable.

Lizzie felt herself growing dizzy as Maxwell Martin walked toward her, grinning.

"See why I wanted you to brush your hair?" Aunt Amanda whispered to Lizzie.

"Bliss, meet Bonita," said Maxwell Martin. He was close enough that Bliss and Bonita could touch noses, and now Lizzie's heart was really pounding. "I think the two of you are going to be good friends."

The dogs stretched out their necks to sniff each other. Lizzie felt Bonita wriggle in her arms.

¡Suéltame! ¡Quiero jugar![9]

"Is there a safe place for them to run around while I do the press conference?" Maxwell Martin asked Aunt Amanda.

[9]*Let me down! I want to play!*

"Press conference?" Lizzie asked.

Aunt Amanda laughed. "That's the big surprise. Maxwell is giving a press conference, for reporters from all the big papers. He'll explain all about organizations like Sato Friends and why they need our support. Plus, he's going to be interviewed by *People* magazine — right here, today. Isn't it fantastic? This will really help spread the word about Satos." As she spoke, several other cars pulled into the parking lot, and people started getting out. "Lizzie, could you take Bliss and Bonita into the playroom? That would be a huge help." Aunt Amanda rushed off without even waiting for an answer.

Dazed, Lizzie just nodded. Maxwell Martin put Bliss on the ground and handed Lizzie her leash. "I've heard all about you, Lizzie. I'm sure you'll take good care of my baby girl," he said. Lizzie nodded again. This was beginning to feel like some sort of weird dream, the kind where you couldn't speak.

A dark-haired woman with a clipboard rushed up to Maxwell Martin. "They're going to be ready for you in a couple of minutes," she said. "Do we need to go over anything?" She reached up and brushed some stray hairs out of his face. "Let me call your hair person over," she said.

Maxwell just grinned. "It's not my first press conference, Nikki." He waved a hand. "Piece of cake. And my hair's fine." He turned to Lizzie. "This is my assistant, Nikki," he said. "Just let her know if there's anything you need."

Lizzie nodded. She was still having trouble speaking, but she forced out the words: "Are you interested in adopting Bonita?" she asked. If Aunt Amanda and Uncle James couldn't keep her, maybe Maxwell Martin would. As a puppy fosterer, Lizzie was always keeping an eye out for the best possible home for every puppy. And what could be better than an exciting, luxurious life with Maxwell Martin? One look at Bliss told Lizzie that this dog was happy and pampered.

Nikki spoke up first. "No way," she said. "One dog is more than enough to keep track of when we're on the road all the time."

Maxwell Martin looked at Nikki. He looked at Lizzie. He looked down at Bonita, and Lizzie thought he seemed a little wistful. He shrugged. "Nikki knows best," he said.

"Nikki knows that your press conference is about to start," said his assistant. She gave Maxwell Martin a little shove toward the cluster of people who were waiting for him.

Lizzie watched as he walked away. Cameras began to whir and flash as several photographers

surrounded him, and reporters yelled out questions. At the last moment, he turned and blew
a kiss.

Lizzie nearly fell over.

"You be a good girl, Miss Bliss," he called.

Lizzie felt herself turn hot all over, and she was
sure her cheeks must be bright red. She could
almost feel Nikki staring at her, and could imagine the smile on her face. Lizzie hid her own face
in Bonita's neck. Of course: the kiss had been for
his dog, not for her. "Let's go, Bliss," she said, tugging on the little dog's leash. "We'll have some fun
playtime while your daddy works."

But before she could head for the playroom,
she heard Maxwell Martin answer a reporter's
question. "Why am I in Littleton?" he asked. "To
promote the Dog-A-Thon, of course. It's all in support of organizations who help dogs like mine,
Satos. Bliss and I wouldn't have missed it for the

world. It'll be a fantastic event. I hope everyone who comes will also buy a ticket for our gala that night."

"Gala?" Lizzie stopped in her tracks and turned to Nikki. "What gala?"

Nikki smiled. "Didn't your aunt have a chance to tell you?" she asked. "Maxwell is so generous. He's agreed to appear at an evening gala — you know, a fancy dress-up event — the night of your Dog-A-Thon. Tickets will be expensive, and all the money will go to Sato rescue organizations."

Lizzie's head was spinning. "Wow," she said.

Nikki checked her clipboard. "There's just one thing," she said. "Maxwell is very busy, and his only available date is this coming Saturday." She peered at Lizzie. "Can I count on you?" she asked. "I know how to plan something like this quickly, but I'm going to need a really good local assistant."

"This Saturday!" Lizzie closed her eyes for a moment. This was crazy. How could they get everything done in just a few days? Then she took a deep breath and nodded. "Of course," she answered.

CHAPTER NINE

"Well, I have to hand it to you, Lizzie." Maria pushed back her hair with a wet, soapy hand. "You may not be so great at crafts, but you sure did a great job planning this event."

It was Saturday, the day of the Dog-A-Thon. Lizzie and her friend had just finished washing a squirmy Lab puppy at the dog-wash station, and both of them were covered in suds.

The part about her not being good at crafts stung, and Lizzie was about to defend herself. Then she remembered her lumpy dog beds. Maria was right about that.

Fortunately, she was also right about the Dog-A-Thon. What a great event. Lizzie smiled as she looked around. The play area at Bowser's Backyard had never looked like *this* before. Colorful booths dotted a midway full of happy people and their dogs. Activity tents had sprung up and were full of eager attendees helping their dogs paw-paint or having their dogs' paws read at the doggy fortune-tellers.

Ms. Dobbins and the rest of the staff of Caring Paws were busy with a steady stream of people interested in adopting dogs. A small stage sat ready for the contests and other entertainment to begin — but first there would be the doggy parade, with celebrity judge Maxwell Martin awarding prizes in categories like Best Costume, Cutest Dog, and Most Spoiled Pup. Later that evening, the indoor play area would be transformed into a sparkling wonderland for the sold-out gala. And it had all come together in less than a week.

"Well, I didn't do it all by myself," Lizzie said. "You all helped, and Nikki was amazing." Maxwell Martin's assistant had turned out to be an incredible organizer. She had helped Lizzie design a poster featuring Maxwell Martin holding Bonita and Bliss, and she had gotten copies printed for free. They had plastered them all over Littleton and the neighboring towns. Lizzie's mom had written a press release for the local newspapers. Nikki and Lizzie had lined up musicians, food vendors, a magician, and sellers of all kinds of cool toys, equipment, and treats for dogs.

"Bonita sure loves the felted ball you made her," Lizzie said, looking down at the little dog by her side. "Don't you?"

Bonita looked up at her, grinning around the big orange-and-red ball in her mouth. She wagged her tail.

¡La estoy pasando buenísimo! Estar con todos estos perros me recuerda a todo lo bueno de vivir en la playa con la jauría.[10]

Despite her bad leg, Bonita had been having a fantastic time all week. Whenever Nikki came to "command central," as Aunt Amanda called the Bowser's Backyard office, where all the planning took place, she brought Bliss along with her. The two dogs had become best friends and could play for hours without stopping — which kept both of

[10]*I'm having a blast! Being around all these dogs reminds me of all the good parts about living on the beach with my pack.*

them out of trouble. When they finally got tired, they would curl up together for a nap, nose to tail and tail to nose. Bonita was worn out at night, so she wasn't driving Aunt Amanda's dogs crazy.

"Has your aunt decided if she's going to keep Bonita?" Maria asked Lizzie.

Lizzie shrugged. "We've been so busy we haven't had the chance to talk about it. I can tell that Uncle James is falling in love with her — I mean, who wouldn't? — but that doesn't mean he'll agree to having five dogs."

Lizzie heard a sudden wave of shouts and screams. "I think Maxwell Martin just arrived," she said to her friend.

"That's what everybody came for," said Maria. "I didn't even know there were this many dog owners around here."

"I know," said Lizzie, craning her neck to try to pick Maxwell Martin out of the crowd that

surrounded him. "I don't care why they're here —
I'm just happy they came. The more people who
come, the more money we raise for Bonita's operation and for all the Satos."

"He's coming this way!" said Maria. She put her
hand over her mouth.

The crowd approached like a tornado, with
Maxwell Martin in the center of a swirling mass
of people: kids asking for autographs, people taking pictures and videos with everything from tiny
phones to full-sized cameras, journalists with
notepads shouting questions. "Poor guy," Lizzie
said, shaking her head. "If that's what it means
to be famous, no thanks."

"Lizzie, he's looking right at us!" Maria said.
Her face turned pink, then white. "I feel like I'm
going to faint."

Lizzie put an arm around her friend. "It's okay,"
she said. "I felt that way, too, the first time I met

him. But he's really nice. You'll see." Lizzie had gotten used to being around Maxwell Martin over the past week. He was just like a regular guy, really.

Maxwell Martin strode right up to their booth with a huge grin. "Bliss had to see her buddy right away," he said. "Plus, I think my girl could use a bath."

He put down the dog he had been carrying in his arms, and Bliss and Bonita touched noses, wagging their tails happily.

¡Hola, amiga! ¿Que pasa?[11]

Neither dog seemed to notice the chaos around them; they were too busy wrestling at the ends of their leashes. Lizzie introduced Maxwell Martin

[11]*Hey, friend! What's up?*

to Maria, and they shook hands. "Your friend Lizzie is a real dynamo," he told Maria.

"I-I know," she said. That seemed to be about all she could manage.

"We'll give Bliss a bath and then she can hang out with us. We'll find you after the contests," said Lizzie.

"Actually, can you keep her until this evening?" Maxwell Martin asked. "I have to leave right after I judge the contests. I have an important errand to do."

Lizzie looked down at Bonita and Bliss, who were tussling happily over Bonita's ball. "No problem," she said.

"You're a peach," said Maxwell Martin. And this time, as he walked away, the kiss he blew really was for Lizzie.

CHAPTER TEN

That night, Lizzie gasped when she walked into the indoor playroom at Bowser's Backyard. "Wow," she said. She'd been with Nikki when they met with the florist, the party rental business, and the caterer, but somehow she had never pictured what it would look like when it all came together. "It's like a fairyland," she said to Aunt Amanda, who stood next to her, beaming. "I never would have imagined it could look this beautiful." Long tables covered in white tablecloths held beautiful china place settings and vases of white and pink roses. Garlands of roses framed a small stage, where some musicians were warming up.

"And all for free," Aunt Amanda said, marveling. "Nikki really has a way of talking people into donating. Now all the money we raise can go to helping Satos."

"What about Bonita's operation?" Lizzie asked. "Don't forget about that."

"Right, right," said her aunt quickly. "Of course. Her surgery is scheduled for next week — and Nikki lined up the best surgeon on the East Coast. Bonita is one lucky girl." She looked Lizzie up and down. "I have to say, you look very beautiful yourself," she added, as if she wanted to change the subject in a hurry.

Lizzie blushed. "Thanks," she said. She was wearing a dress, which was unusual for her, and she felt weirdly girly — in a good way. Her mom had bought the dress as a surprise and left it on her bed. Lizzie had found it when she dashed home to shower and change between the afternoon and evening events. It was a cool dress, a retro paisley print in wild pinks and oranges. Lizzie spun around, showing her aunt how the skirt flared.

"Very nice," said her aunt. "I'm sure Maxwell Martin will like it."

Lizzie felt her cheeks growing even hotter. "Why would I care?" she asked.

Her aunt held up her hands. "Just kidding," she said. "Where is he, anyway? People are arriving, and they're going to expect the show to start soon." She checked her watch. "He should have been here a half hour ago."

Aunt Amanda went to try to track him down, and Lizzie found her seat at a table near the front. Daphne, Brianna, and Maria were already sitting there, and they were all dressed up, too. "Woo-hoo," said Maria when Lizzie sat down. "You look great."

Lizzie began to wish she'd just worn her normal clothes. She felt self-conscious and awkward, even around her best friends. Why did people like to dress up, anyway? She sat quietly, watching the room fill up. Everybody was chatting, and the noise level in the room rose and rose. Still, Maxwell Martin had not arrived.

"Where is he?" Daphne asked. "Maybe he found something more important to do."

"Or maybe he just forgot," Brianna said. "But I don't think so. He was so nice when he came to our booth. He bought two dog beds and two balls. I almost fainted when he smiled at me."

"Two beds?" Lizzie asked. That was odd. But she didn't have any time to wonder about it, because just then the noise in the room rose to a roar. She craned her neck to watch Maxwell Martin arrive, trotting into the room with an apologetic smile on his face. Nikki strode beside him, carrying her clipboard, as always.

Maxwell Martin shook hands and signed quick autographs as he moved through the crowd. When he leapt onto the stage, everyone started to applaud. He held up his hands. "Thanks, mates," he said with his adorable accent. "We'll get started right away, but first I want to explain why I'm late. I just bought a house in Littleton!"

The place went wild. Applause, hooting, and happy shrieks greeted his statement.

"I fell in love with this town as soon as I saw it," he said. "I've been looking for a peaceful home base, and I've found it. I'll be proud to be your neighbor."

More hooting and hollering.

Maxwell Martin grinned and threw kisses at the crowd. Throwing kisses was just his thing,

Lizzie realized. She shrugged, smiled, and threw a kiss back at him, the way everyone else was.

Maxwell turned to his band. "And a-one, and a-two," he counted, and at the very first notes, the audience cheered. Maxwell grinned. "You all know this song, I think," he said into the mic. "And I think a lot of you know the dance, too. Come on up if you do!" He waved his hands invitingly, and people began to head for the stage.

Maria turned to Lizzie. "Let's go!" she said. They jumped up, along with Brianna and Daphne, and squeezed into a few spots at the front of the stage.

"Every day is my birthday," they sang along with Maxwell Martin. *"Every day everything is new."* They threw their hands in the air and wiggled their heads. Lizzie could not stop smiling. She was having a blast.

"Every day a new day to spend it all with you," she sang at the top of her lungs as she did the quick side-to-side step of the dance.

"Every day a new day to spend it all with you!" everybody finished a few moments later. The cymbals crashed and the band played the last chord. "Wooo-hooo!" Lizzie yelled, throwing her hands in the air along with everybody else.

Maxwell Martin laughed and applauded. "Great job, everybody," he said. They left the stage and found their seats. Lizzie's heart was beating hard.

It beat even harder when Maxwell Martin leaned into the microphone. "By the way, ladies and gents," he said, "you were being filmed. I think you may see yourselves online in a few days."

"Whoa! We're going to be in one of his videos," Brianna said.

"Pretty cool," said Lizzie.

"Can somebody bring Bliss and Bonita out, please?" Maxwell asked, looking offstage.

A moment later, Aunt Amanda walked out with the two dogs and handed their leashes to Maxwell. He bent down and scooped them both into his arms. "Awwww," went the crowd.

"These two beautiful Satos have become such good friends," said Maxwell Martin. "I've decided I can't separate them, so . . . I'm going to adopt Bonita."

There was a huge round of applause, but Lizzie was almost too shocked to clap. Before she had a moment to think, Maxwell made another announcement.

"Of course, as Bonita's owner, I am responsible for her medical bills," he said. "That means that every cent of the money raised at today's Dog-A-Thon and tonight's gala will go toward helping

Satos who are still on the island. Congratulations to all of you!"

At that, all the audience members leapt to their feet and gave Maxwell Martin a standing ovation. He smiled and held both dogs up to his face, kissing each in turn. Bonita's little tail wagged with happiness as she licked her new owner's cheek.

¡Te amo muchísimo! ¡Gracias![12]

"Such great news," Maria yelled into Lizzie's ear.

Of course it was. Bonita would love living with Bliss, in the center of all the activity and excitement that was Maxwell Martin's life — but Lizzie couldn't help wondering how Aunt Amanda felt.

[12]*I love you very much! Thank you!*

She looked up at the stage and met her aunt's eyes. Aunt Amanda grinned at her and gave her a thumbs-up. Of course she was happy. Lizzie realized that this news was not a surprise to her aunt: Maxwell Martin must have talked it over with her. And Bonita and Bliss would probably both come to Bowser's Backyard all the time now that they were neighbors — so Lizzie would get to see them, too.

Lizzie grinned back at her aunt. Then she turned to her friend. "It is," she said to Maria. "It's the best news ever."

PUPPY TIPS

There are organizations all over the world that help stray dogs. Many people learn about Satos when they visit Puerto Rico, and some even adopt Satos and bring them home — but there are still more dogs than homes. Sato rescue organizations have their hands full trying to save these scrappy stray mutts. You can learn more about how to help by searching Sato dogs online, with a parent's help.

Dear Reader,

I have never met a Sato, but have heard many stories about people who adopted dogs they met and fell in love with when they were vacationing at a beach spot — in Puerto Rico, Mexico, or other places. These dogs often have amazing stories, and turn into beloved and loyal pets. I always wanted to write about a Sato, and it was fun to research the topic and then bring Bonita to life. I love her sassy attitude and fun-loving personality.

Yours from the Puppy Place,
Ellen Miles

P.S. If you enjoyed Bonita's personality and want to read about other sassy dogs, try DAISY or RASCAL.

"No batter, no batter!"

Charles Peterson glared at the guy sitting next to him in the stands. Why was he yelling that? The man standing at the plate, waving a bat around as he waited for a pitch, happened to be Charles's father. Dad might not be the best softball player in the world, but Charles knew that he could hit: they played all the time in the backyard and even went to the batting cages together some-times. "Home run, Dad!" he shouted over the guy's heckling. "Go for it!"

The man next to Charles grinned and shrugged. "All in good fun," he said. "My brother's a cop, so I have to root for them."

The softball game was an annual spring event in Littleton: firefighters against police. Charles went every year, and of course he always rooted for the firefighters, since his dad was part of the Littleton Fire Department.

Unfortunately, the firefighters always lost.

So far.

Maybe, thought Charles, *this would be their year.* "My dad's a firefighter," he told the man.

The man nodded. "Good for him," he said. "And hey, it looks like they have a chance this time."

It was true. They were in the top of the ninth inning, and the police still had not scored a run.

The firefighters hadn't, either, but now they had two runners on base. Charles knew them both: Meg was on first, and Rick, one of the newer guys on the squad, was on third. "Bring 'em home, Dad," Charles yelled as the pitcher wound up. He knew that the police would still have a chance to score when they came up for the end of the inning, but a couple runs would be great insurance.

"Yup," said the man as the ball sailed over the plate, "they've got a chance, as long as Reggie doesn't show up."

"Steeerike!" yelled the ump.

Charles's dad stepped back from the plate, frowning and shaking his head.

"Reggie?" Charles asked. "Oh, right. Reggie. The guy who gets all the home runs." Now he remembered. Reggie was the main reason the police won every year. He was a state trooper, big and muscular. He could hit to just about any spot in the field, and he could field, too. He usually played third base. Sure enough, Charles saw that there was a new guy at third, an unfamiliar face. Definitely not Reggie. That was good news.

Charles's dad stepped back in, took his stance, and got ready for the next pitch. Charles had a feeling he was going to swing hard this time— but he didn't. The pitch came in low, and the umpire called, "Ball!"

"One and one," said the man next to Charles.

The next pitch was a ball, way to the outside. "Ball two," called the ump.

Charles's dad swung hard at the next pitch but didn't make contact. He kicked the dirt. Charles could tell he was frustrated. Another pitch, high and inside, and the count was full. "Come on, Dad," Charles said under his breath. "Come on!"

The pitcher wound up. She let the ball fly.

Charles's dad stepped in, swung hard, and connected! The ball went sailing deep into left field. Charles jumped to his feet. "Yes!" he yelled when he saw the ball bounce to the ground between the two guys who'd been running for it. "Go, Dad," he shouted as he watched his dad sprint for first. Already Rick had crossed home plate. Now Meg was between third and home, and Dad was rounding second. Out in the left, a player swept the ball up in his glove, bobbled it, recovered, and threw hard to the third baseman.

ABOUT THE AUTHOR

Ellen Miles loves dogs, which is why she has a great time writing the Puppy Place books. And guess what? She loves cats, too! (In fact, her very first pet was a beautiful tortoiseshell cat named Jenny.) That's why she came up with the Kitty Corner series. Ellen lives in Vermont and loves to be outdoors with her dog, Zipper, every day, walking, biking, skiing, or swimming, depending on the season. She also loves to read, cook, explore her beautiful state, play with dogs, and hang out with friends and family.

Visit Ellen at www.ellenmiles.net.